Teachers, librarians, and kids from across Canada are talking about the *Canadian Flyer Adventures.* Here's what some of them had to say:

I love the fact that these are Canadian adventures—kids should know how exciting Canadian history is. Emily and Matt are regular kids, full of curiosity, and I can see readers relating to them.  ~ *JEAN K., TEACHER, ONTARIO*

## What kids told us:

I would like to have the chance to ride on a magical sled and have adventures.  ~ *EMMANUEL*

I would like to tell the author that her book is amazing, incredible, awesome, and a million times better than any book I've read.  ~ *MARIA*

I would recommend the *Canadian Flyer Adventures* series to other kids so they could learn about Canada too. The book is just the right length and hard to put down.  ~ *PAUL*

The books I usually read are the full-of-fact encyclopedias. This book is full of interesting ideas that simply grab me.  ~ *ELEANOR*

At the end of the book Matt and Emily say they are going on another adventure. I'm very interested in where they are going next!  ~ *ALEX*

I like when Emily and Matt fly into the sky on a sled towards a new adventure. I can't wait for the next book!  ~ *JI SANG*

# Halifax Explodes!

## Frieda Wishinsky

Illustrated by Patricia Ann Lewis-MacDougall

MAPLE
TREE

For my cousin and friend Philippe

Many thanks to the hard-working Owlkids team, for their insightful comments and steadfast support. Special thanks to Patricia Ann Lewis-MacDougall and Barb Kelly for their engaging and energetic illustrations and design.

Maple Tree books are published by Owlkids Books Inc.
10 Lower Spadina Avenue, Suite 400, Toronto, Ontario M5V 2Z2
www.owlkids.com

Library and Archives Canada Cataloguing in Publication

Wishinsky, Frieda
Halifax explodes! / Frieda Wishinsky ; illustrated by Patricia Ann
Lewis-MacDougall.

(Canadian flyer adventures ; 17)
Issued also in an electronic format.
ISBN 978-1-926818-97-9 (bound).--ISBN 978-1-926818-98-6 (pbk.)

1. Halifax Explosion, Halifax, N.S., 1917--Juvenile fiction.
I. Lewis-MacDougall, Patricia Ann II. Title. III. Series: Wishinsky,
Frieda. Canadian flyer adventures ; 17.

PS8595.I834H35 2011          jC813'.54          C2011-905276-8

Library of Congress Control Number: 2011935671

E-book ISBN: 978-1-926818-99-3

 Canada Council    Conseil des Arts      ONTARIO ARTS COUNCIL
for the Arts    du Canada              CONSEIL DES ARTS DE L'ONTARIO

We acknowledge the financial support of the Canada Council for the Arts,
the Government of Canada through the Canada Book Fund, the Ontario
Arts Council, and the Ontario Media Development Corporation.

Manufactured by Friesens Corporation
Manufactured in Altona, MB, Canada in August 2011
Job# 67868

A     B     C     D     E     F

# CONTENTS

# HOW IT ALL BEGAN

Emily and Matt couldn't believe their luck. They discovered an old dresser full of strange objects in the tower of Emily's house. They also found a note from Emily's Great-Aunt Miranda: "The sled is yours. Fly it to wonderful adventures."

They found a sled right behind the dresser! When they sat on it, shimmery gold words appeared:

*Rub the leaf*
*Three times fast.*
*Soon you'll fly*
*To the past.*

The sled rose over Emily's house. It flew over their town of Glenwood. It sailed out of a cloud and into the past. Their adventures on the flying sled had begun! Where will the sled take them next? Turn the page to find out.

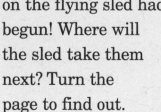

# 1

# Surprise

*Ping. Ping. Ping.*

Ice pellets bounced off Emily's living room windows.

"I hate icy days," said Emily. "You can't make snow people. You can't play outside. You can't do anything good."

"You can do something good inside," said her friend Matt. He pointed to the floor above them.

"Of course!" said Emily, bouncing out of her chair. "Why didn't I think of that? We can go on a sled adventure."

"So, what are we waiting for?" said Matt.

Emily and Matt raced out of the room and up the back stairs to the tower room.

"Why don't we make this one a surprise adventure?" suggested Matt. "One person can pick the drawer."

Emily's eyes lit up. "And the other person can pull something out of it with eyes closed!"

Matt smiled. "I like that idea, but that means we could go anywhere at any time in history. It could be..."

"Dangerous?" said Emily.

"Yes."

"Or fun?"

"Yes."

"Or both," said Emily.

Matt nodded. "So...let's do it! I'll pick the drawer."

"And I'll pull out the surprise adventure."

"I pick drawer...number four!" Matt pulled open the bottom drawer.

Emily bent down. She closed her eyes and fumbled inside the drawer.

"Here it comes," she said. "One. Two. Three. Out!"

She yanked out a thin, flat object.

"It's a photograph," said Matt as Emily opened her eyes.

The friends stared at the photograph of a smiling girl of ten dressed in a winter coat, boots, a scarf, and a hat. On her lap sat a small spotted dog.

"That dog is cute," said Emily, "but there's no label telling us who the girl is, or where they are, or what year it is. There's always a label."

"Maybe there's something on the back of the picture," said Matt.

Emily turned the photograph over. "You're right! It says:

*Dear Tim,*
*This picture is part of your birthday present. Can you guess the rest?*
*Love, Carolyn and Poppy*
*Dec. 6, 1917, Halifax, Nova Scotia.*

"Let's go! I love surprises and I love cute dogs. I wish I could pet him right now!" said Emily.

"He looks like a friendly dog, but I bet there's more to this adventure than a surprise present and a dog. The sled always sends

**4**

us somewhere where something awesome is happening."

"You're right. But what's awesome about Halifax in 1917?" asked Emily.

Matt rubbed his fingers across his forehead. "Let me think. The end of World War I was near 1917. Maybe this has something to do with the war."

"Did the war take place in Halifax?"

"No. In Europe, but something must have been going on in Halifax. Something important. I'm sure of it," said Matt.

"There's only one way to find out," said Emily as she pulled the sled out from behind the dresser.

## 2

# What was *That?*

Emily and Matt hopped on the sled.

"I have my sketchbook. Do you have your digital recorder?" asked Emily.

"Of course!" said Matt as the shimmery gold words appeared on the front of the sled.

*Rub the leaf*
*Three times fast.*
*Soon you'll fly*
*To the past.*

Emily rubbed the leaf and immediately fog enveloped the sled. Soon they were flying above Emily's house and above Glenwood, and heading toward a fluffy white cloud.

They zoomed out of the cloud and looked down.

As they did, they heard a loud blast.

The sled shook. "Yikes!" screamed the friends, grabbing the sides of the sled.

"What was *that?*" asked Emily.

Matt swallowed hard. "I don't know, but I can smell smoke. I was sure we were going to fall off the sled."

"Look! I see the smoke. Something terrible has happened down there—but what?"

"I don't know, but we're heading right toward it. This is scary. I wish we could turn the sled around."

Emily gulped. "Yeah! Go somewhere else, sled. Please!"

But the sled just kept going down.

"Oh no! Look at the city. It looks like a bomb hit it. Houses are crushed. Buildings are on fire. And there's a huge wave rolling in from the ocean. It's hitting everything. This is horrible," said Emily, shivering.

"Maybe it *is* the war. Maybe it did come to Halifax," said Matt. "But why would there be a wave?"

"I don't know. All I know is that the sled

is turning!" said Emily. "Where are we going to land?"

For a minute the friends said nothing. They held on tightly to the sides of the sled as it flew lower and lower.

"We're heading for that hill," said Emily, pointing. "Phew! It doesn't look like it's been hit. Maybe we'll be safe."

Matt shuddered. "But what will we see

when we get to Halifax? What's happened to the city? What happened to Carolyn, Tim, and Poppy? What kind of adventure is this, anyway?"

The sled thumped down onto the ground. Emily and Matt hopped off the sled and looked around. People were hurrying up the hill. There was no sign of a girl who looked like Carolyn.

"Brrr—it's cold," said Emily. "At least we're dressed for winter."

Emily was wearing a long red coat, high boots with buttons, a scarf, and a small hat. Matt was wearing a green jacket, a cap, and boots.

"Look. Over there!" Emily pointed to a spot not far from where they were standing.

A small spotted black and white dog was wandering around. His leash was dangling and his fur was dirty.

"Do you think that could be Poppy?" said Emily.

"Come on," said Matt. "Let's call him by that name and see."

Matt pulled the sled behind him as the friends dashed over to the little dog.

As they neared him, he began to bark.

"It's okay, Poppy," said Matt as they drew closer. "We won't hurt you."

But the dog kept barking.

"Maybe it's not Poppy, or maybe the blast just scared him," said Emily. She reached out toward the small dog and touched his back gently. "It's okay. We're friends," she said. "You're safe now."

# 3

# Poppy

The little dog stopped barking and licked Emily's hand.

"It *is* Poppy!" said Emily. "Look! His name is on his collar."

"He likes you," said Matt. "You're good with dogs."

Emily smiled. "I've been asking for a dog for my birthday forever. I'd love a dog like Poppy. But where's Carolyn and where's Tim?"

The friends looked around the hill. More people were rushing up.

"It's so smoky. It's hard to breathe up here. Imagine what it must be like down there," said Matt.

Emily shuddered. "I don't want to think about it. Let's look for Carolyn. Maybe Poppy can lead us to her. Maybe we can help her. Maybe that's why the sled brought us here."

"But where should we start? We have to find out what happened in the city first. Let's ask that woman in the blue coat over there." Matt pointed to a woman near them who was peering out toward the city. Her face, hair, and coat were covered in soot. "She looks familiar."

Emily nodded. "She does—but how would

we have met her before? She probably just looks like someone we know."

Emily held Poppy's leash, and the friends hurried over to the woman.

"Could you tell us what happened?" Emily asked.

"I don't know," said the woman. "All I know is that there was an enormous blast near the harbour. Some people think the Germans have invaded Halifax, but we don't know for sure."

"Is your family okay?" asked Matt.

"Luckily we live far from the harbour in the south end of town. Our windows were shattered. There's dust, glass, and soot everywhere, but my family is fine. I took them to a safe spot far from the harbour. But I had to come here and find out what happened. So many people have been injured...or worse."

The woman put her hands over her face

and began to sob. Then she cleared her throat and pulled a handkerchief out of the pocket of her coat. She wiped her eyes. "You must excuse me. This has been a terrifying day. You children must be frightened, too. Is your family safe?"

"Yes. We're all safe," said Matt.

"How did you find Carolyn's little dog?" asked the woman. She bent over and petted the small animal.

"You know Carolyn and Poppy?" asked Matt.

"Carolyn lives next door to me," said the woman.

"Poppy was wandering around here on his own. We didn't see anyone with him," said Matt.

"Oh dear. I hope nothing has happened to that poor child. I've known her since she was a baby. The windows at her house were shattered, but I didn't think anyone inside was hurt." Tears filled the woman's eyes again. She quickly wiped them away.

"Look," said Emily, "more people are running up the hill."

"Everyone believes that Citadel Hill is the safest place in the city," said the woman. "And there are rumours of another blast. Maybe worse than the first one."

Emily gulped. She stared at Matt. His face had turned white at the mention of another explosion.

What was going to happen next?

# 4

# I Know You!

"You know, you two look very familiar," said the woman. "Are you from around here?"

"No," said Emily.

"Then you're visiting. I hope your family is far away from Halifax," said the woman.

"Very far," said Matt.

"Good," said the woman as even more people hurried up Citadel Hill. "Someone has to know what happened. I can't believe that this is the second disaster I'm living through. How did I manage to survive the *Titanic* and this terrible day, too?"

"Oh my goodness," Emily blurted out. She looked at Matt and he nodded. Now they knew why the woman looked familiar. They'd met her on the *Titanic*. She'd shown them her wedding dress just before the *Titanic* hit the iceberg. And when it hit, they'd told her to rush to a lifeboat. But luckily she didn't remember where she'd seen them. If she had, it would have been hard to explain what they were doing in Halifax and why they didn't look a day older than when she'd met them in 1912— five years ago!

"In all the confusion, I forgot to introduce myself," said the woman. "My name is Mrs. Hilda Slayter Lacon. What are your names, children?"

Emily took a deep breath. "I'm Emily and this is Matt."

"Emily and Matt," repeated Mrs. Lacon. "I met two children with those names on the *Titanic*. It's strange, but you look so much like them." Mrs. Lacon shook her head. "My memory must be playing tricks on me. With all that's happened, I'm not thinking straight. How could you be the same two children?"

"That would be..." said Emily.

"Impossible," said Mrs. Lacon. "But for a minute I could have sworn you were the children I met on that terrible night at sea. I'm sure you heard about the *Titanic*."

"Yes," said Matt.

"It's a miracle I was able to get on a lifeboat that night, and now it's a miracle that the blast happened far from my home. But we must find out what's going on. We must see what we can do to help. I only know one thing for sure. Nothing will ever be the same in Halifax after this day."

"Mrs. Lacon?"

Mrs. Lacon spun around. A tall young soldier approached them. His brown hair was white with soot and his uniform was dirty and torn.

"Tim!" she cried, hugging the solider. "I'm so glad that you're all right. These two children, Emily and Matt, found Poppy. But they haven't found your sister. Is she with you?"

"No. I'm looking for Carolyn. She was walking Poppy before school, but she never made it to school. Our family is frantic."

"Oh, my poor boy. You must find her. Do you know what happened in the city? Have the Germans invaded Halifax?"

"The Germans haven't invaded. It was a terrible accident. My buddy from the army saw everything. He ran to our house to see if we were all right. He said that two ships—the *Imo* and the *Mont-Blanc*—collided in the harbour. No one knew that the *Mont-Blanc* carried explosives. Now the harbour and many neighbourhoods have been destroyed." Tim shuddered. "I have to find my sister."

"We'll help you," said Matt.

"I bet Poppy can help, too," added Emily.

"I must return to my family," said Mrs. Lacon. "Please let me know as soon as you can if dear Carolyn is safe. And take care of yourselves, too. These are dangerous times."

# 5

# The Photo

"I've brought this to help me find Carolyn," said Tim, pulling a photo out of his pocket.

It was the same photo that Emily had pulled out of the dresser!

"Today is my birthday," said Tim. "Carolyn had the photo made for me. She wrote on the back that she had another present for me, too. It was supposed to be a surprise. This whole day *has* been a surprise—a terrible one."

Tim bit his lip and rubbed his eyes. Emily and Matt knew he was trying not to cry.

"We'll find her. I know it," said Emily. She patted Tim on the back.

"Let's go," said Tim. "I know Carolyn's dog walking route. Someone must have seen her this morning."

Emily and Matt followed Tim down Citadel Hill. Emily held Poppy's leash and Matt carried the sled.

The air was thick with smoke as they passed a house whose windows had all been shattered. A woman sat outside on a broken chair. She stared out into the distance shaking her head and saying over and over, "I can't believe this. How did it happen?"

"Excuse me," said Tim. "But have you seen this girl?" Tim showed her the photograph of Carolyn and Poppy.

"Yes. I know that girl," said the woman. "She always walks her dog down this block.

I see her when I sweep my porch. She has a nice smile and always says hello."

"Did you see her today?" asked Emily.

"Yes. I saw her fifteen minutes before the blast. Poor girl. I hope she's well." The woman shook her head again. "Such a terrible day. So many hurt. So many—" Then she stared off into the distance.

"Poor woman," said Tim. "She's in shock."

"But at least we know Carolyn was around here not long before the blast. She couldn't have walked too far," said Emily.

"I hope not," said Tim. "I was afraid she might have run down to the harbour. Many people hurried down there after the ships first collided. There was a spectacular fire and people were curious. No one knew the ships would explode."

The group trekked on. As they passed a small house with broken doors and windows, they heard moans coming from inside.

"Look!" said Emily. "Part of the roof has fallen in."

"They're people inside who need help!" said Tim. "I have to go in and see what I can do. You two stay here."

Emily, Matt, and Poppy waited outside. Tim carefully climbed over the broken front door.

They heard him call to the people inside. Then they heard someone cry out, "Come, quickly!"

Soon Tim was back out, carrying a boy of about seven. His mother hobbled out after him.

Tim placed the boy gently on the ground. "This is Andrew. I think his leg is broken," said Tim. He grabbed a piece of ripped curtain and a small board, and made a splint. "This will do for now, but we need to get him seen by a doctor. Camp Hill Hospital isn't far from here. Let's take him there. We can ask at the hospital about Carolyn. And if she's not there, we'll hurry back here to look some more."

"We can put Andrew on the sled and pull him," said Matt.

"Good idea," said Tim. "I don't think I can carry him all the way."

# 6

# Is She Here?

The hospital was only a few blocks away. It was packed with injured people. Some hobbled in on their own. Some leaned on a friend, a relative, or a stranger. Some were carried in on makeshift stretchers or in people's arms. Doctors and nurses scurried around trying to help as many people as they could.

Tim found a stretcher and carefully lifted Andrew off the sled and onto it.

"Go find your sister," the boy's mother told Tim. "Andrew will be fine. Thank you all for

your kindness. We're the lucky ones." The woman sighed. "So many are worse off today."

"Let's look around the hospital for Carolyn," said Matt.

"We could ask a nurse or a doctor if they've seen her," said Emily.

Tim nodded. It was hard to move around the hospital with so many people coming in and so little space for the wounded. They tried not to get in the way of the doctors and nurses dashing from patient to patient. It was hard to stop a doctor or nurse to ask about Carolyn. Finally, Tim tapped a doctor on the shoulder.

"What is it, young man?" barked the doctor. "I don't have time to talk."

"My sister is missing. Have you seen her, sir?" Tim showed the doctor Carolyn's photograph.

"No. I haven't seen that girl, but so many people have passed through here today that it's hard to remember faces." The doctor sighed. The expression on his face softened. He touched Tim's arm gently. "Now, if you'll excuse me, I have to tend to the wounded. I hope you find your sister."

"Thank you, sir," said Tim.

Tim, Emily, Matt, and Poppy walked up and down the wards packed with the wounded. But there was no sign of Carolyn anywhere. They showed her picture to other nurses and doctors, but no one had seen her.

Then they went outside. Tim slumped into a broken bench in front of the hospital. He choked back tears.

"We can't give up," said Emily. "We have to keep looking."

"Let's go back to that first house where the woman saw Carolyn before the blast," said Matt.

Tim took a deep breath. Then he stood up. "You're right. There's no time for sadness now. We have to keep looking. We have to find her— and we will."

They hurried down the streets, back toward the first house where they'd helped Andrew. As they passed it, they spotted a thin, grey-haired man sitting on a legless couch outside a house. The roof of his home had caved in. The man stared at a picture of his family.

"Excuse me, sir," said Tim. "Do you need help?"

The man looked up. "Thank you, young man. My family is safe. That's all that matters. My house can be repaired."

Tim pulled out Carolyn's photo from his pocket. "Have you seen this girl? She's my sister."

The man examined the photo carefully.

"I haven't seen the girl, but I have seen that hat. Look over there and you'll find it. The hat was such a bright shade of red that I couldn't forget it."

The man pointed to a pile of debris in front of a house nearby. "Good luck," he said.

# 7

# Carolyn's Tree

Tim raced to the pile. It was a tower of broken beds, ripped clothing, broken glass, and parts of windows and doors. Just as the man had said, there on top lay a red hat. Carolyn's hat.

Tim picked it up and wiped the dust and dirt off. "She was here—or somehow her hat blew over here."

"She's probably close by right now," said Emily.

Just then Poppy began to bark and pull at his leash.

"Poppy knows that it's Carolyn's hat," said Tim. "He loves her. He barks for an hour every day after she leaves for school."

"But which way should we look for her now?" asked Matt.

"Carolyn usually walks to the right," said Tim. "There's a big old tree she loves that way. It has four large branches and beautiful pink blossoms in the spring. It's right near Mrs. Winter's Candy Store. Carolyn calls it her tree."

The children followed Tim. The explosion had hit the stores and houses on this block hard. Building walls had caved in. Roofs had blown off.

"Carolyn's tree has to be here. I was sure I'd recognize it. It has such an unusual shape but so many of the trees have been damaged," said Tim. "Nothing is the same." He took a deep breath. "I have to find Carolyn. She's a terrific girl. I...I...want you to meet her."

"I know we'll meet her soon," said Emily.

"Is Carolyn's scarf red, like her hat?" asked Matt.

"Yes!" said Tim.

"Well, there's a red scarf beside that tree over there." Matt pointed to a large tree. Two of its branches had fallen against the wall of a house.

"That's her scarf!" said Tim, running over to the tree. "I bet this was her tree, although it's hard to recognize it in this condition. She must be around here somewhere."

"Look!" said Emily. "There's a sign on that broken building. It says, 'Mrs. Winter's Candy Store'."

"Poor Mrs. Winter. Her store was special. All the children loved it. It was Carolyn's favourite place."

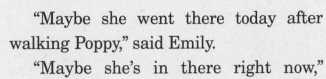

"Maybe she went there today after walking Poppy," said Emily.

"Maybe she's in there right now," said Matt.

Just then a woman stumbled out of the damaged candy store.

"My store...my store," she muttered.

Tim, Matt, and Emily hurried over to the woman.

"Sit down," said Matt, dragging over a chair that had survived the explosion. They helped the woman to the chair.

"Mrs. Winter, are you hurt?" asked Tim.

"My head aches terribly," said Mrs. Winter. "I fell against a counter. Look at my store. What happened?"

"The whole city has been damaged in a terrible explosion," said Tim.

Mrs. Winter looked up at Tim. "I know you. You're Carolyn's brother. She was just talking to me about you before that terrifying blast."

Tim swallowed hard. "Do you know where Carolyn is right now?"

"No. She left the store about five minutes before everything happened. It was all so quick. The noise. The smoke. The shaking. Everything falling. Everything breaking."

Tears trickled down Mrs. Winter's face.

She wiped her eyes with her hand and looked up at Tim. "She was buying gumdrops for your birthday, Tim. It was going to be a surprise. She was walking her dog when she stopped by. I told her she'd better hurry to school. I told her she'd be late. And then...then...

"Find her, Tim. You must."

# 8

# Waiting for Tim

"Gumdrops were the surprise! So that was what the words meant on the back of the photograph!" said Tim. "I'll never forgive myself if anything happens to Carolyn. I'm going to look in the store just to be sure."

Matt and Emily glanced at each other. They were both thinking the same thing. What if Carolyn wasn't there? What if Carolyn was hurt—or worse?

"You two stay outside with Poppy," said Tim. "Make sure Mrs. Winter is all right."

"Maybe Poppy can help you find Carolyn," Emily suggested.

"I don't want anyone else going in with me. The store doesn't look safe. A wall could fall down any minute. I'll be back as soon as I can."

With that, Tim stepped over the broken front door and the shattered glass.

"Be careful," Emily and Matt called out.

The two friends and Poppy waited outside. They listened for voices from inside the building but they heard nothing. Mrs. Winter sat quietly in the chair, moaning and sighing.

"Are you okay?" asked Matt.

"My head still hurts but I'll be fine," she said. "I'm just worried about that sweet girl. Her brother survived the war to come home to this terrible business. It's all horrible."

"I can hear Tim calling Carolyn now," said Emily.

"Listen!" said Matt.

They heard a clunk, as if something hard had been dropped.

"Oh no. No. No," Tim groaned.

Emily and Matt looked at each other. Was Tim hurt? Had he found Carolyn?

"Here comes Tim!" cried Emily.

Tim climbed over the broken front door. His hair was streaked black and white with soot and dust. There was a large hole in the sleeve of his uniform. His scratched face was bleeding.

"What happened?" Matt asked.

"I didn't find Carolyn," said Tim. "I walked all the way to the back of the store and looked around. I called out for her over and over. I looked everywhere. I looked under everything—broken glass, broken beams, bashed-up counters, piles of boxes. But she wasn't there."

Mrs. Winter walked over to Tim. "You're bleeding, my boy," she said. She pulled a handkerchief out of her pocket and pressed it against Tim's face. "Hold it steady there for a bit," she said.

"I'll be fine. I cut myself on some glass," said Tim. "I have to keep looking."

"Maybe Carolyn went down the street behind the store," suggested Emily.

"You could be right," said Mrs. Winter. "There's a little park down that block. You can reach it from the lane that runs beside the store. Dogs love that park. Maybe Carolyn took Poppy there."

"I'm going to look right now!" said Tim.

"Can we come with you this time?" asked Matt. "Carolyn might be stuck under something. It would be easier if you didn't have to move or lift things alone."

"Poppy can help, too," said Emily. "I bet he'll know when we're near Carolyn."

Tim nodded. "It's hard to do this alone. But please be careful. There's sharp debris everywhere. Let's go."

As they stepped over a pile of bricks in front of the lane, Poppy began to bark. With each step Poppy barked louder and louder.

"Poppy knows something," said Emily.

"I'm sure of it."

"There's a large mound of broken glass coming up," Tim said. "Watch your step."

"I'm picking Poppy up and carrying him," said Emily. "I don't want him to get cut."

The three friends stepped over the glass. They stepped over bricks, beams, and broken crates. They walked on and on down the dark narrow lane. They were close to the end of the lane.

"Ouch!" screamed Emily.

# 9

# Down a Dark Lane

Tim and Matt turned around.

"I tripped over some of the rubble, but I'm fine. Let's keep going," said Emily.

Soon they could see the little park. Tree branches had toppled over on bushes. Benches were broken. It was a jungle of twigs and branches.

"Wait," said Matt. "I hear something."

"H-here," said a small voice.

"Carolyn!" shouted Tim. "Is that you? Tell us where you are."

"Help. Please!"

"Where are you?" asked Tim, looking around. "I can't see you. Can you describe where you are?"

"Hurry...please," was the only response.

"What do we do now?" asked Matt.

"Follow Poppy," said Emily. "Look at the way he's leaning. I think he wants us to look near that tree," she added, pointing to a big old tree. Two of its large branches had come down in the blast. "I bet Carolyn's near there."

"Let's go," said Tim.

The three friends climbed over a jumble of twigs, sharp pine needles, and jagged branches.

"Help! Tim, I'm here!"

"I can hear you, Carolyn," shouted Tim. "We're coming. We're close to you now."

Suddenly Poppy leaped out of Emily's arms and ran over to the fallen branches. He stood beside them and barked.

"Carolyn, are you under these branches?" asked Tim.

"I'm under a bench. The tree fell on it. My ankle and arm hurt."

"Carolyn! I see you!" shouted Tim. "We're going to get you out. We're going to get you help. We just have to move the two big branches."

Matt and Tim tried to lift the larger branch, but it was so heavy they couldn't budge it.

"Let's try again," said Tim. "One. Two. Three. Lift!"

They still couldn't move it.

"Let me help," said Emily.

Emily picked Poppy up and placed him down on a small patch of soil. "Don't move," she said.

As if he understood the importance of what she was asking, the little dog didn't budge.

Emily, Matt, and Tim each held on to a

different part of the branch.

"One. Two. Three. Lift!" said Tim.

The three friends huffed as they tried to pull the branch up and away from the bench. Slowly, slowly, it began to move. Slowly, slowly, they lifted it up and over.

Then they moved the second branch. Now they could see Carolyn! Her arm was bruised and her ankle was swollen. Tim lifted the broken pieces of the bench away from his sister. Then he wrapped his arms around her. Poppy bounded over and licked her face.

"I was so scared we wouldn't find you," said Tim.

"I thought I'd be stuck here forever," said Carolyn. "I knew you'd look for me if you could, Tim. I went to the candy store to buy your favourite gumdrops for your birthday. I still have them in my pocket."

Tim smiled for the first time since Emily and Matt had met him. "I'll have some gumdrops later. But finding you is the best birthday present. And meeting Emily and Matt is wonderful. They've taken care of Poppy and helped me find you. Can you walk?"

"I don't know. My ankle hurts a lot."

"I'll carry you," said Tim. He lifted his sister up.

"We can pull Carolyn on our sled to the hospital," said Emily.

"The sled! Oh no!" said Matt. "We can't. I don't remember where it is. We may have left it—"

"At the hospital!" said Emily.

"Yes!" said Matt.

"Don't worry. I can carry Carolyn. She's not heavy," said Tim. "I'm sure you'll find your sled there. But if you don't, it's just a sled. I'm sure you can get another one."

Matt gulped. "Not like this one."

# 10

# Where's the Sled?

Tim carried Carolyn. Emily and Matt followed
with Poppy. As soon as they arrived, Matt and
Emily peered around the entrance hall of the
hospital. No sign of the sled.

"Do you remember where you last saw it?"
Emily asked Matt.

"We had it when we were helping Andrew.
Then we were so busy rushing around looking
for Carolyn that we must have forgotten about
it. Andrew could be anywhere. The sled could
be anywhere."

The hospital overflowed with people. Doctors, nurses, and volunteers raced around bandaging people and offering them food and water.

"Please help my sister," said Tim to a nurse.

The nurse quickly examined Carolyn's arm and leg. "You're a lucky girl. Nothing is broken. You have a nasty bruise on your arm and your ankle is sprained. If you can get some ice, put it on your ankle right away. Keep your leg up. Rest and you'll be fine. I have to go now."

"Thank you! That's a relief! I'm going to take Carolyn home," said Tim. "Our parents will be so happy to see her." He turned to Emily and Matt. "Thank you both for your help. When things are better, come and visit us."

"We wish we could," said Emily.

"But we probably have to leave Halifax and we don't know when we'll be back," said Matt.

"Thanks for looking out for Poppy," said Carolyn. "Would you like some gumdrops before I go?"

Emily and Matt shook their heads. They patted Poppy. "He's a sweet dog," Emily told Carolyn. "Goodbye, Poppy."

Matt and Emily waved as Tim and Carolyn left the hospital.

"I like Carolyn. It would have been fun to get to know her," said Emily.

"We'd better find our sled," said Matt.

"Let's look for Andrew. Maybe the sled is still there beside him."

The friends walked up and down the long halls of the hospital. They looked up and down for the sled and Andrew, but they didn't see either.

"What are we going to do now?" said Matt after they'd checked all the rooms and halls.

"I can't think straight anymore," said Emily. "It's so sad to see all these hurt people. Let's go outside."

"I hope no one tossed the sled in the garbage," said Matt, as they headed to the front door of the hospital.

"They couldn't. They wouldn't. The sled wasn't broken or anything. It has to be here somewhere."

They reached the main door leading outside

the hospital. In front of the door, they saw a girl of ten pulling a boy of five on a sled.

"Hey, Em!" said Matt. "It's our sled."

Emily's eyes lit up. "Where did you get that sled?" she asked the girl.

"It was lying around. This boy went home and left it," said the girl.

"It's our sled," said Emily. "We brought that boy to the hospital on it."

"Oh," said the girl. "Come on, Peter. Let's give these children back their sled."

"No," said Peter. "I like this sled, Mary. We found it. It's ours now."

"It's not your sled. We need it. Come on, Peter. Give it back," said Emily.

But Peter wouldn't budge.

"Come on, Peter," said Mary. "It belongs to these children. It's not ours. Mama will be angry if we don't give it back."

"I don't care," said Peter. He started to cry.

"I'm sorry. Peter is upset because our grandmother was hurt in the explosion."

"We understand," said Matt, patting Peter on the back. "But we really need the sled back."

Peter wiped the tears out of his eyes with his hand and shook his head.

Mary sighed. "Well, there's one good way to get Peter off that sled." She leaned over and whispered into Emily and Matt's ears.

"Okay," said Emily. "Let's do it."

"One. Two. Three. Tickle attack!" said Mary.

Mary, Emily, and Matt tickled Peter under his chin, under his arms, and behind his ears.

"Cut it out," he said, giggling.

But the three wouldn't stop till Peter squirmed off the sled.

Matt grabbed the sled, and the two friends raced out the front door of the hospital.

"Thanks, Mary!" they called.

"Quick. Let's hide before Peter tries to find us," said Matt.

"No time to hide," said Emily. "Look at the sled."

*You came in time*
*To help a friend.*
*Your journey now*
*Is at an end.*

Emily and Matt hopped on the sled. As soon as they did, the sled flew up over the hospital, over Halifax, and into a fluffy white cloud.

Soon they were back in Emily's tower.

The friends slid off the sled.

"Phew! We were lucky to find the sled," said Emily.

"But, boy, that was a surprise adventure," said Matt. "I'd never heard anything before about that terrible explosion in Halifax. I want to find out more."

"Me, too," said Emily. "Let's check on the Internet, but first I want some gumdrops."

"Gumdrops? You said no to Carolyn when she offered you some."

"That's 'cause I didn't want to eat gumdrops that had been through an explosion. There could have been dirt on them, or who knows what."

"Do you have any gumdrops at your house?"

"I have a bag in our candy drawer. I got some for Halloween. I ate all the red and green ones, but I think there are some blue ones left. They might be squished, though. I sat on the bag by accident," said Emily.

"Squished gumdrops?" said Matt. "Yuck."

"When they're squished, the flavour is even better," said Emily. "Really. Try some."

"No, thank you. You can have them all."

Emily smiled. "Great! I will."

# MORE ABOUT...

After their adventure, Matt and Emily wanted to know more about Halifax, the explosion, and the aftermath. Turn the page for their favourite facts.

# Emily's Top Ten Facts

**1.** Railway worker Vincent Coleman hurried to his telegraph office to warn two incoming trains about the explosion. He sent this telegraph: *Hold up the train. Ammunition ship afire in harbor making for Pier 6 and will explode. Guess this will be my last message. Good-bye boys.*

**2.** Coleman died in the explosion but his courage and warning saved 700 lives.

Wow!
What a hero!
—M.

**3.** As the French ship, the *Mont-Blanc*, exploded, its anchor was blown five kilometres (three miles) away from the harbour while its cannon was blown in the opposite direction.

**4.** The Halifax Explosion caused such a big tsunami (wave) that the cargo ship *Imo*, which had collided with the *Mont-Blanc*, was lifted onto shore.

**5.** Glass flew everywhere in the explosion. Windows were broken as far as 80 kilometres (50 miles) away.

**6.** Right after the explosion, thousands of people in Halifax gathered on Citadel Hill to find out what happened.

**7.** Everyone was afraid that the Germans had attacked. Eventually Canadian troops showed up and told them there was no more danger.

**8.** Artist Arthur Lismer, who later became famous as a member of the Group of Seven painters, was in Halifax during the explosion and drew pictures of what he saw.

**9.** Hilda Slayter Lacon was born in Halifax and survived the Titanic disaster in 1912. She later came back to Halifax with her son Reginald when her husband enlisted to fight in World War I.

Hilda was lucky again!
—M.

**10.** Hilda lived in the southern part of the city, which wasn't as badly damaged as the north.

# Matt's Top Ten Facts

1. Halifax was important in World War 1 because it has a deep harbour with a wide entrance, making it one of the world's best harbours to anchor a ship.

2. A ship is supposed to raise a red flag if it's carrying explosives.

3. The captain of the *Mont-Blanc* didn't raise a red flag because he didn't want the Germans to know that the ship was carrying explosives.

4. The *Mont-Blanc* burned for 20 minutes as it drifted toward Pier 6 in the north end of Halifax.

5. Crowds gathered on the pier to watch the fire. They had no idea the ship would soon explode.

6. People as far away as Prince Edward Island and New Brunswick felt the vibrations of the tsunami that hit after the explosion.

7. Over 1,600 homes and an entire Mi'kmaq tribe encampment were completely destroyed in the explosion.

8. The captain, pilot, and five crewmembers of the *Imo* died in the explosion. One crewmember of the *Mont-Blanc* died. The *Mont-Blanc*'s captain had ordered everyone to abandon ship when the fire broke out.

9. After the explosion, the *Imo* was repaired, renamed, and launched again. It sank in December 1921 after hitting a reef in the South Atlantic Ocean.

10. Almost 2,000 people died in Halifax in the explosion.

I'm glad we found Carolyn and helped her. —E.

# So You Want to Know...

## FROM AUTHOR FRIEDA WISHINSKY

When I was writing this book my friends wanted to know more about what happened to Halifax and its people after the explosion. I told them that although all the characters in my story, except Hilda Slayter Lacon, were made-up, the story is based on the real events of that terrible day in Halifax on Thursday, December 6, 1917.

Here are the questions I answered.

### How quickly did people get help after the explosion?

Within 30 minutes after the explosion, people organized search-and-rescue teams to bury those who'd died and to help the injured and homeless. A relief committee was set up, too, but on Saturday a blizzard blanketed the city and work slowed. After the storm died down, heavy rain drenched everything. Then the temperature fell and the rain froze. It was a horrible mix of events and weather, and it made life miserable. It also made conditions for rescue and help difficult.

## Did other cities and countries come to help Halifax?

Help came from many Canadian cities and countries around the world, including the United States, England, Australia, China, France, South America, and New Zealand. Expert engineers and salvage workers arrived, too. New York held a Halifax Relief Day, and Chicago cabled money.

But the most memorable effort came from the city of Boston. As soon as news of the explosion reached Boston, a train was loaded with supplies. The next day another train left for Halifax full of supplies, medical personnel, and equipment for a hospital. Two ships carrying supplies also sailed, though they were delayed by the terrible weather. To this day the citizens of Halifax send Boston a large Christmas tree every year as a thank you for all the help and support.

## Did the explosion have any positive after-effects?

Doctors learned more about treating patients in the open air during emergency situations. That knowledge helped improve medical treatments, hospital facilities, and social welfare services. Harbour regulations also became stricter to avoid disasters like the Halifax Explosion in the future. Scientists began to study the ocean floor to learn more about the effects of man-made and natural disasters. A Halifax housing development called the Hydrostone was built of fireproof concrete blocks for people who lost homes in the explosion. It was a design innovation and is still used today.

## Was anyone blamed for the accident?

A week after the explosion an enquiry began into what happened and who was responsible. The captain and pilot of the *Mont-Blanc* were charged with manslaughter, but the charges were dropped because it was hard to know for certain who was really to blame for all the mistakes made. In May 1919, the Supreme Court of Canada said that both ships, the *Mont-Blanc* and the *Imo*, were equally to blame for the disaster.

## Are there any memorials to the Halifax Explosion?

There are many gravestones and monuments to the Halifax and Dartmouth victims (the neighbouring city of Dartmouth also suffered terrible damage). A large Memorial Bell Tower stands on Fort Needham overlooking the site of the explosion. The tower bells are rung every December 6 at 9 a.m., and a service is held to honour those who died and suffered in the tragedy. The bells can be heard across Halifax and Dartmouth.

Teacher Resource Guides now available
online. Please visit our website at
**www.owlkids.com**
and click on the red maple leaf to
download tips and ideas for using the
series in the classroom.

# The *Canadian Flyer Adventures* Series

**#1 Beware, Pirates!**

**#2 Danger, Dinosaurs!**

**#3 Crazy for Gold**

**#4 Yikes, Vikings!**

**#5 Flying High!**

**#6 Pioneer Kids**

**#7 Hurry, Freedom**

**#8 A Whale Tale**

**#9 All Aboard!**

**#10 Lost in the Snow**

**#11 Far from Home**

**#12 On the Case**

**#13 Stop that Stagecoach!**

**#14 SOS! Titanic!**

**#15 Make It Fair!**

**#16 Arctic Storm**

**#17 Halifax Explodes!**

# More Praise for the Series

"[Emily and Matt] learn more than they ever could have from a history textbook. Every book in this new series promises to shed light on a different chapter of Canadian history."
~ *Montreal Gazette*

"Readers are in for a great adventure."
~ *Edmonton's Child*

"This series makes Canadian history fun, exciting and accessible."
~ *Chronicle Herald (Halifax)*

"[An] enthralling series for junior-school readers."
~ *Hamilton Spectator*

"...highly entertaining, very educational but not too challenging. A terrific new series."
~ *Resource Links*

"This wonderful new Canadian historical adventure series combines magic and history to whisk young readers away on adventure...A fun way to learn about Canada's past."
~ *BC Parent*

"Highly recommended."
~ *CM: Canadian Review of Materials*

# About the Author

Frieda Wishinsky, a former teacher, is an award-winning picture- and chapter-book author, who has written many beloved and bestselling books for children. Frieda enjoys using humour and history in her work, while exploring new ways to tell a story. Her books have earned much critical praise, including a nomination for a Governor General's Literary Award. She is the author of *Please, Louise; You're Mean, Lily Jean; Each One Special;* and *What's the Matter with Albert?* among others. Originally from New York, Frieda now lives in Toronto.

# About the Illustrator

Patricia Ann Lewis-MacDougall started drawing as soon as she could hold a pencil, and filled every blank spot in her mother's cookbooks by the age of three. As she grew up, Pat Ann never stopped drawing and enjoyed learning all about the worlds of animation and illustration. She now tells stories with her love of drawing, and has illustrated children's books and created storyboards for television animation for shows such as *Little Bear* and *Franklin the Turtle*. Pat Ann lives in Stoney Creek, Ontario.